SACRAMENTO PUBLIC LIBRARY

040

D0622659

CENTRAL LIBRARY
828 "I" STREET
SACRAMENTO, CA 95814
SEP - 2000

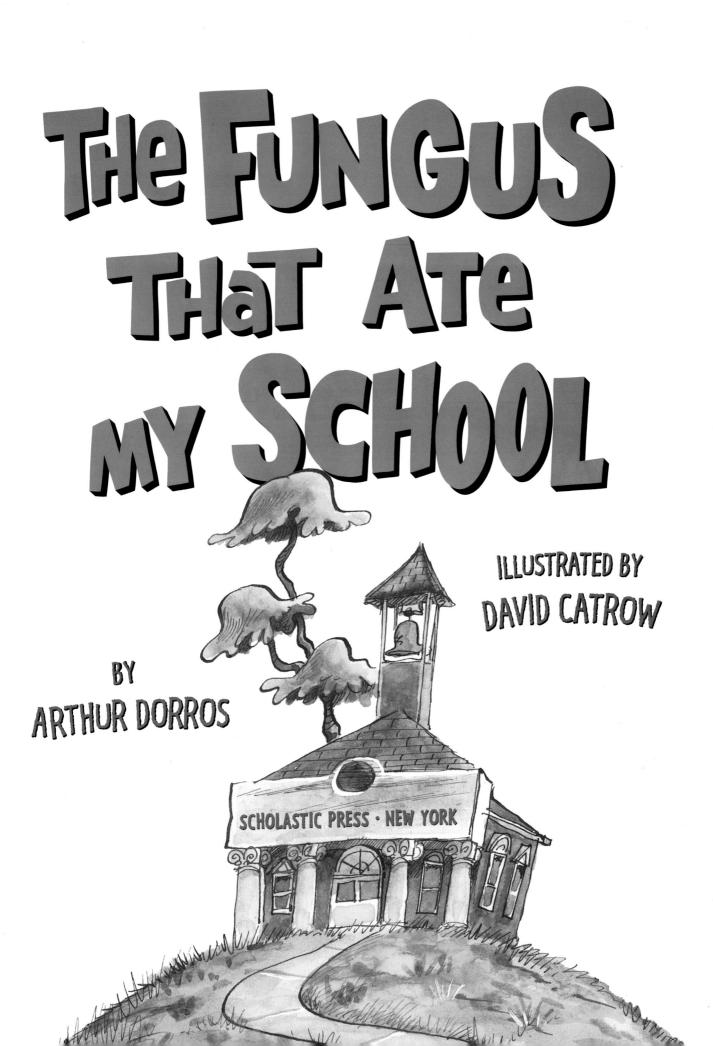

THE FUNGUS THAT ATE MY SCHOOL

BY
ARTHUR DORROS

ILLUSTRATED BY
DAVID CATROW

SCHOLASTIC PRESS · NEW YORK

AUTHOR'S NOTE: Fungi are a part of people's everyday lives. For example, those critical in Earth's "recycling" help make soil. Can a fungus really eat a school? No. But every year, schools and other buildings develop fungus infestations. These problems happen when tiny fungi spores, bits of fungi, find the right conditions to grow. Tiny bits of fungi are almost everywhere — in air, water, wherever living things can exist. They will not grow enough to become problems without the right environment, such as on wet or damp materials in a building. If you have questions about fungus infestations, consult a fungus expert — who could be a "mycologist," someone who specializes in studying fungi, or someone at an environmental inspection firm.

Text copyright © 2000 by Arthur Dorros

Illustrations copyright © 2000 by David Catrow

All rights reserved. Published by Scholastic Press, a division of Scholastic Inc., *Publishers since 1920.*

SCHOLASTIC and SCHOLASTIC PRESS and associated logos are trademarks and/or registered trademarks of Scholastic Inc.

No part of this publication may be reproduced, or stored in a retrieval system, or transmitted in any form or by any means, electronic, mechanical, photocopying, recording, or otherwise, without written permission of the publisher. For information regarding permission, write to Scholastic Inc., Attention: Permissions Department, 555 Broadway, New York, NY 10012.

Library of Congress Cataloging-in-Publication Data

Dorros, Arthur.

The fungus that ate my school / by Arthur Dorros ; illustrated by David Catrow. — 1st ed.   p.   cm.

Summary: While the students are home for spring vacation, the fungus they are growing in their classroom grows and grows and takes over the entire school.   ISBN 0-590-47704-8   [1. Fungi—Fiction. 2. Science —

Experiments—Fiction. 3. Schools—Fiction.] I. Catrow, David, ill. II. Title.

PZ7.D7294 Fu   2000   [E] — dc21   99-25350   CIP

10 9 8 7 6 5 4 3 2 1   0/0 01 02 03 04

Printed in Singapore 46

First edition, April 2000

Book design by David Caplan

The text type was set in 18-point Kosmik-Plain Three.

The illustrations in this book were rendered in watercolor and gouache.

To Debbie, and to Alex and Ellen,
who aren't anything like the characters in this book,
except that Alex found a fungus and something ate Ellen's homework
— A.D.

To Debbie (you've really grown on me) with love
— D.C.

We told Mr. Harrison our science experiments
were getting out of control.
He didn't believe us,
until IT ate our school.

CAUTION
CRAYFISH

IT started before spring vacation.
Our class was studying fungus.
We were growing fungus in jars.
"Are you sure our experiments will be all right
while we're not here?" we asked Mr. Harrison.
"Don't worry," he told us,
"fungus can take care of itself."

There was rain during the whole vacation.
Our first day back at school,
Ms. Moreover, the principal,
opened the front doors early.
"Come on, children, let's get out of the rain."

We walked into the dark hallway.
Ms. Moreover turned on the lights.
"AAAG!" yelled Ellen.
Green, yellow, and purple fuzz
covered everything.
"What is IT?" asked Ms. Moreover.
"IT's big and ugly," said Ellen.
"IT's fantastic!" I said.
"IT is *not* fantastic," said Ms. Moreover.
"That's true, IT's a fungus!" said Mr. Harrison.

The bell rang.

Actually, the bell went *thud, thud, thud.*

IT had smothered the bell.

The slimy fuzz covered the floors, walls, bulletin boards, even the lights.

"**IT**'s eating everything!" I said.

"I don't hear **IT** chewing," Ellen noted.

"I didn't think fungus had a mouth," said Alex.

"Look! **IT**'s eating our universe!" cried Ellen.

IT squished under our feet
as we tromped down the damp hallway.
Water splattered on our heads.
"The roof's been leaking," Mr. Harrison said.
"That's definitely a problem," said Ms. Moreover.
She opened the office door.
"**IT** has taken over my office!"

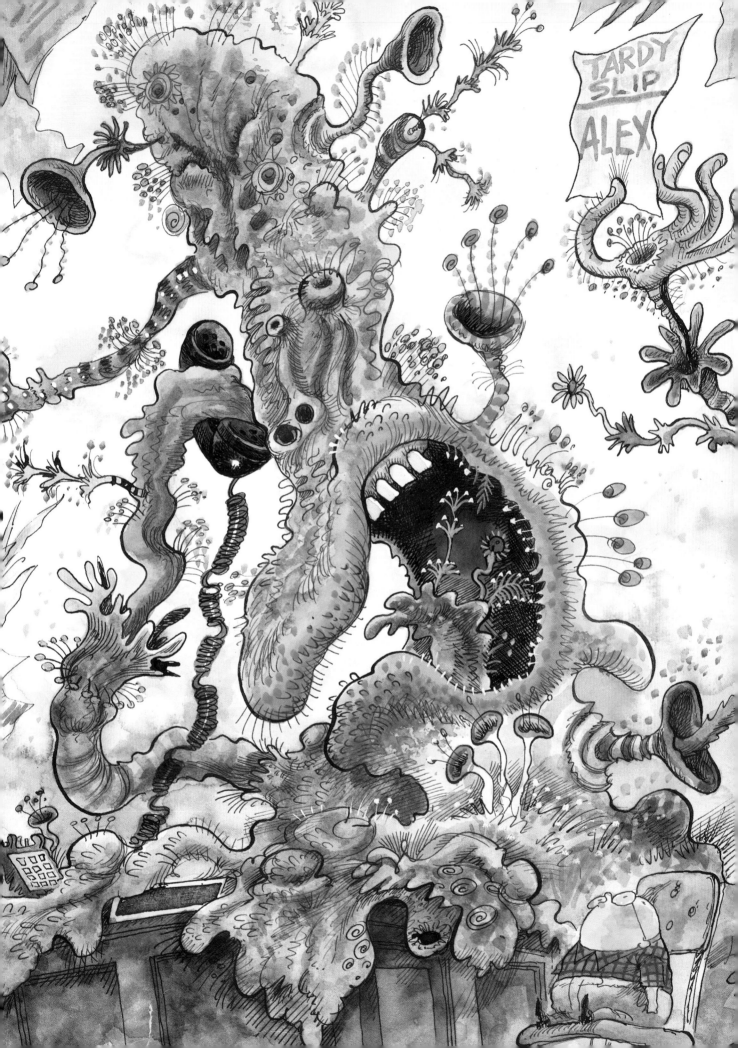

We ventured further through the dark halls.
Mr. Page, the librarian, looked into the library.
"Oh, no," said Mr. Page.
He fainted.
End of Page.

Mr. Harrison let us into our classroom.
"IT ate my notebook!" called Alex.
"IT's eating my homework!" cried Ellen.
"Just as I thought," said Ms. Moreover
when she saw the jars of fungus we'd been growing.
"IT must be one of your class's experiments."
"IT doesn't look like mine," I said.
"We need an expert opinion," said Mr. Harrison,
"I know just who to call."

We went to the cafeteria.
"Don't let **IT** eat the food!" said Ms. Moreover.
Too late.
"Looks like **IT** can eat almost anything," I said.
"Quickly children, run!" said Ms. Moreover,
"I mean *walk* to the nearest exit."

TODAY'S MENU
TUNA LEUCOCEPHALUM
PEACHES SPORANGIA
GREEN BEAN EPIDENDRUM
BROWNIE
SOUR MILK

PAY HERE

A car pulled up.
"Professor Macademia is here," Mr. Harrison said,
"she knows fungus."
"She looks like she knows fungus," said Ellen.
"Amazing," said Professor Macademia,
"IT's a jewel, a treasure!"
"How can we get rid of IT?" Ms. Moreover asked.
"That's all I want to know."

"Fresh air, light, elbow grease, and a little help
from my friends in the Fungus Unit
ought to get rid of IT," said Professor Macademia.
"Fungus Unit? What's a Fungus Unit?" Ellen asked.
"Special branch of the Sanitation Department,"
said someone dressed in white,
pulling a giant hose into the school.
Other workers carried in shovels, mops, and big lights.
"Action!" called one of them.
Suddenly the whole school was filled with
whirring and clanking, swooshing and scrubbing.

The Fungus Unit scraped IT off of everything
in the school and hauled IT away.
Professor Macademia kept our fungus experiments.
"I want to see if one of them is IT," she said.
She held up one of the fungus jars.
"Aha!" said Professor Macademia. "This is IT!"
"It's not mine," said Alex.
"Uh-oh," I said. "IT's mine."
"IT's not your fault," said Professor Macademia.
"The wet, closed-up school was the perfect place
for a fungus to grow.
You have made a great discovery!
This fungus belongs in the Museum of Fungus and Industry."

OUR
Golden
Moldy

Our class got a special award from the museum.

"Congratulations, class," Ms. Moreover said.
"However, Mr. Harrison, I think you've learned
enough about fungus for now."
"Don't worry," said Mr. Harrison.
"No more fungus experiments —

— until next year."